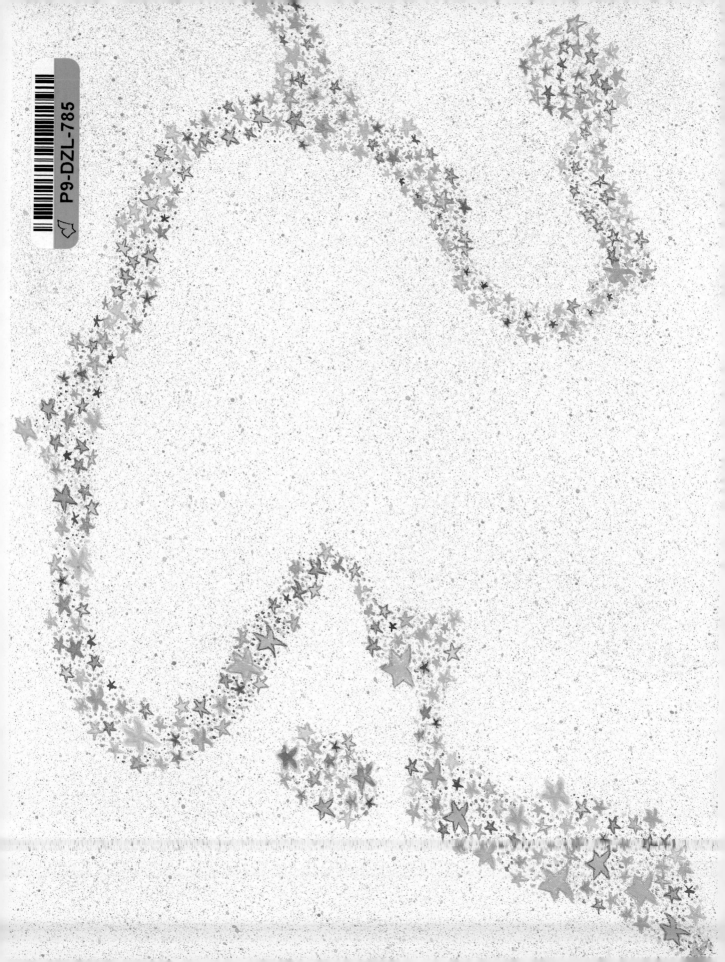

Copyright © 1997 Kim Hansen
Snuggletime Companion Bedtime Stories
is a registered trademark of Kim A. Hansen

Published by Gloria Magnus Publishing, Inc.
P.O. Box 6792
Arlington, Virginia 22206
United States Of America
703-548-5985

ISBN 0-9652474-1-4
Library of Congress Catalog Card Number 97-93096

Summary: Two snuggletime bears think up excuses to
postpone their bedtime!

Printed in China by Palace Press International

This book
is
lovingly dedicated
to our
Precious Sweetie Pies,
Leslie & Julie
for their everlasting
imagination and inspiration
throughout the daytime
and
remarkably at bedtime!
Confectionately yours,
Mommy & Daddy

Good night my precious Sweetie Pies,
It's time to go to sleep.
I beg of you to close your eyes,
Tucked safe beneath the sheets.

Don't bother to procrastinate,
Let's just turn out the light.
If you start to confabulate,
We will be up all night.

You understand it's time for bed,
So why must you resist?
Please gently rest your weary heads,
Here is my good-night kiss.

But, Mommy, Daddy we're not tired,
We're really wide awake.
The problem is we have acquired
The habit, "Stay up late!"

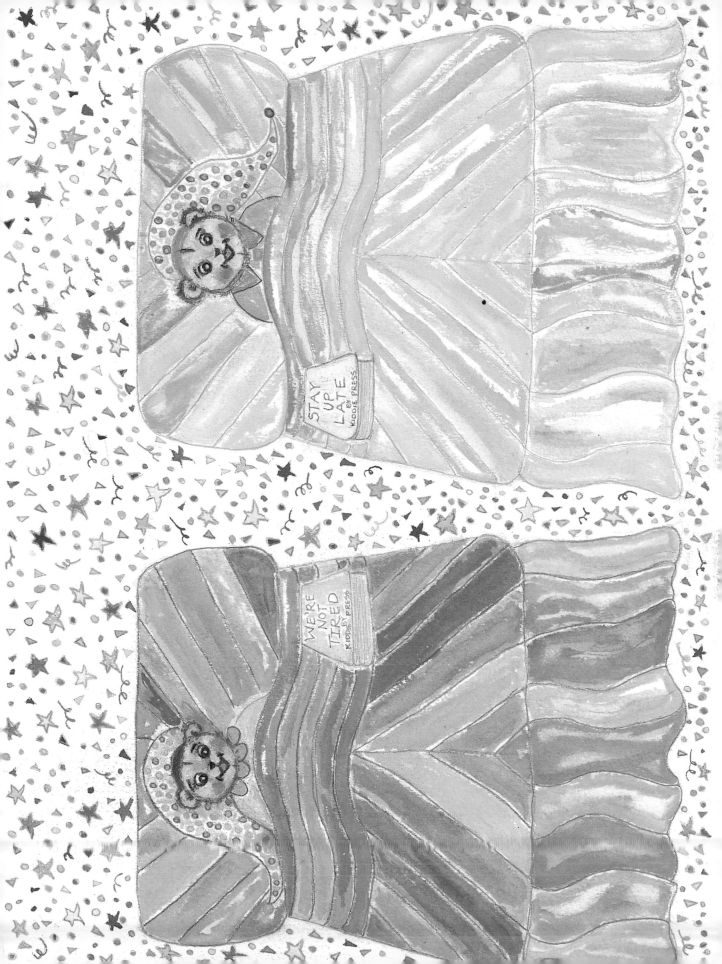

Good night my precious Caramels,
My actor; my actress.
Tonight, I hope you won't retell
Your numerous requests.

Each night in bed you plead and cry
"I didn't get dessert!"
If that won't work, I know you'll try
"I think my tummy hurts."

Perhaps you'll say, "My mouth is dry,
I really need a drink."
Before I finish my reply,
You're skipping towards the sink.

But, Mommy, Daddy we appeal,
Our tummies really ache.
If only we could strike a deal
To have more chocolate cake.

Good night my precious Angel Cakes,
What will you think of next?
Why do you want to stay awake?
Your parents are perplexed.

It's getting late my clever kids,
The clock is ticking fast.
I can't believe what time it is,
This dallying can't last!

But, Mommy, Daddy you had said
That we could watch TV.
One show before we go to bed,
We hope you will agree!

Instead, we'll watch a video.
A short one, please say yes.
When it's all done, then we will go
To sleep, as we promised.

Good night my precious Jelly Rolls,
Tonight so full of glee,
Your lack of sleep will take its toll
And make you contrary.

You've had your drink. You've had your show.
You've had your dessert, too.
Don't ask for more, we'll just say no
To further gripes from you!

But, Mommy, Daddy, we can't cease
From bouncing up and down
Until you read one bedtime piece
With a melodic sound.

Tomorrow, we'll pick up our clothes,
Clean up our jillion toys.
We'll stack our blocks in tidy rows,
Like darling girls and boys!

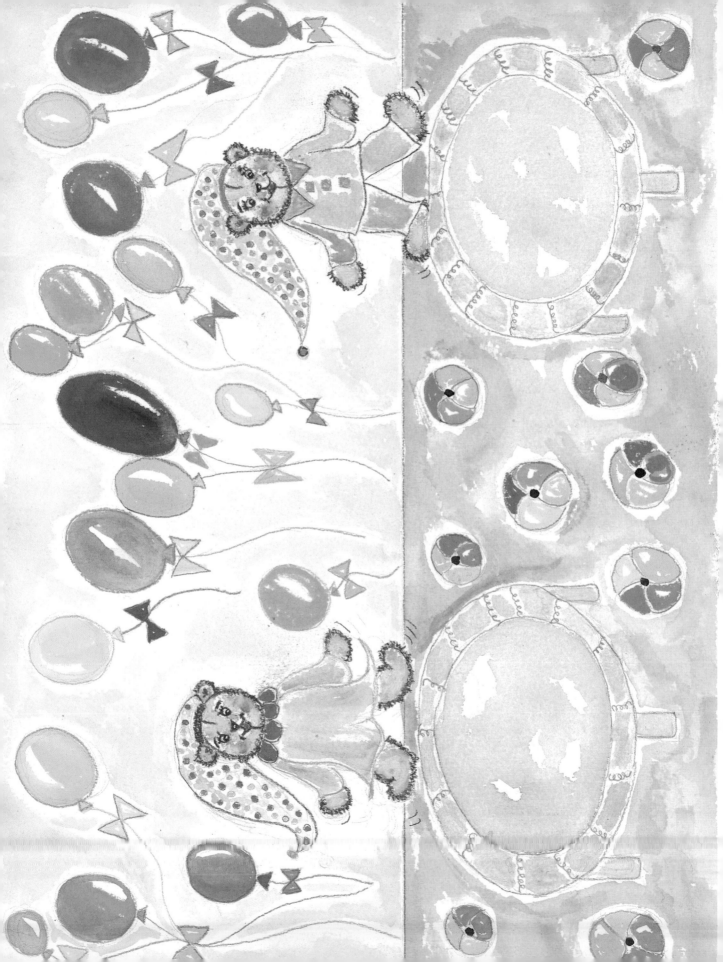

Good night my precious Sugar Plums,
I'll read one nursery rhyme,
A lovely lullaby that's fun,
For the one millionth time!

Remember, I will read just one,
And not another word.
Swiftly to sleep when I am done;
These late nights are absurd.

But, Mommy, Daddy can we sit
Upon our reading chair?
We can't unwind, we're filled with zip,
We're peppy teddy bears.

Because we love the time we spend
With you, our biggest fans,
We promise we will make amends
And go to sleep as planned.

Good night my precious Peach Flambèes,
I've finished with your rhyme.
Have you exhausted all the ways
To postpone your bedtime?

But, Mommy, Daddy we forgot
To take our bathtime soak.
We are not asking for a lot,
Your patience we invoke.

Could we please have our rubber ducks,
Toy soldiers, swimming fish?
We guess we shouldn't press our luck
And ask for one more wish.

While we are in our soapy tubs,
We'll need your company.
We want to shower all our love
On Mommy and Daddy.

Good night my precious Jubilees,
Let's dry your soaking heads.
Here is tonight's last hug and squeeze,
Now waltz back to your beds.

Beguiling schemes you try on us.
You're such professionals.
Please go to bed without a fuss,
And stop these obstacles.

But, Mommy, Daddy now we're scared
To be all by ourselves.
What happens if a monster stares
Out from behind our shelves?

We wish we had a bright nightlight
To help us to be brave.
We'll finally fall asleep tonight,
We promise to behave.

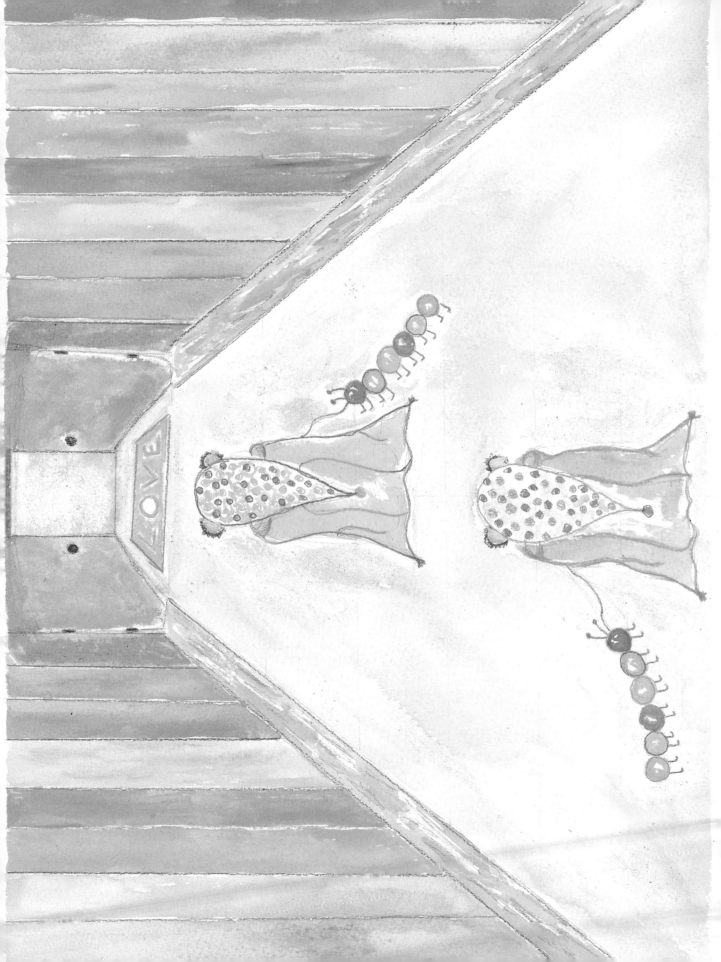

Before, you asked us to recite
Your favorite bedtime rhyme.
But now you want a bright nightlight,
What will it be next time?

Perhaps you are insomniacs;
When will the chatter cease?
Please kindly try to just relax,
Your parents both want peace!

But, Mommy, Daddy our hearts ache
For you throughout the night.
From you we cannot separate,
We tried with all our might.

OK, you win just for tonight,
You may sleep in OUR bed.
I love you, please turn out the light.
Sweet dreams, my sleepy heads.

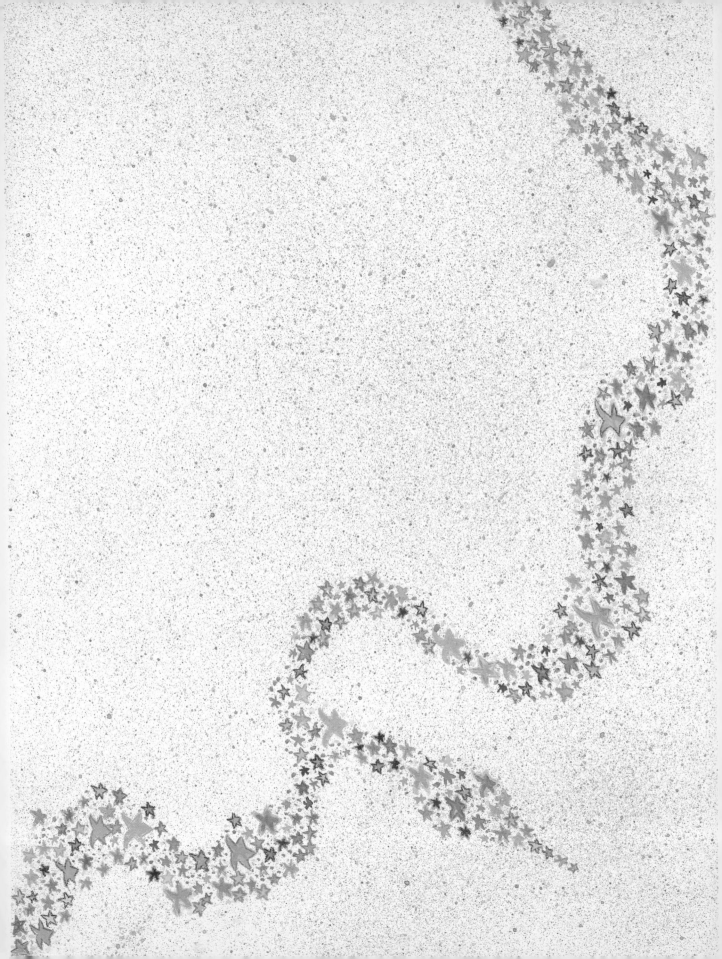